Dedicated to my children:
Isaiah, Kiera, and Alexa

And their Mother… Dokka

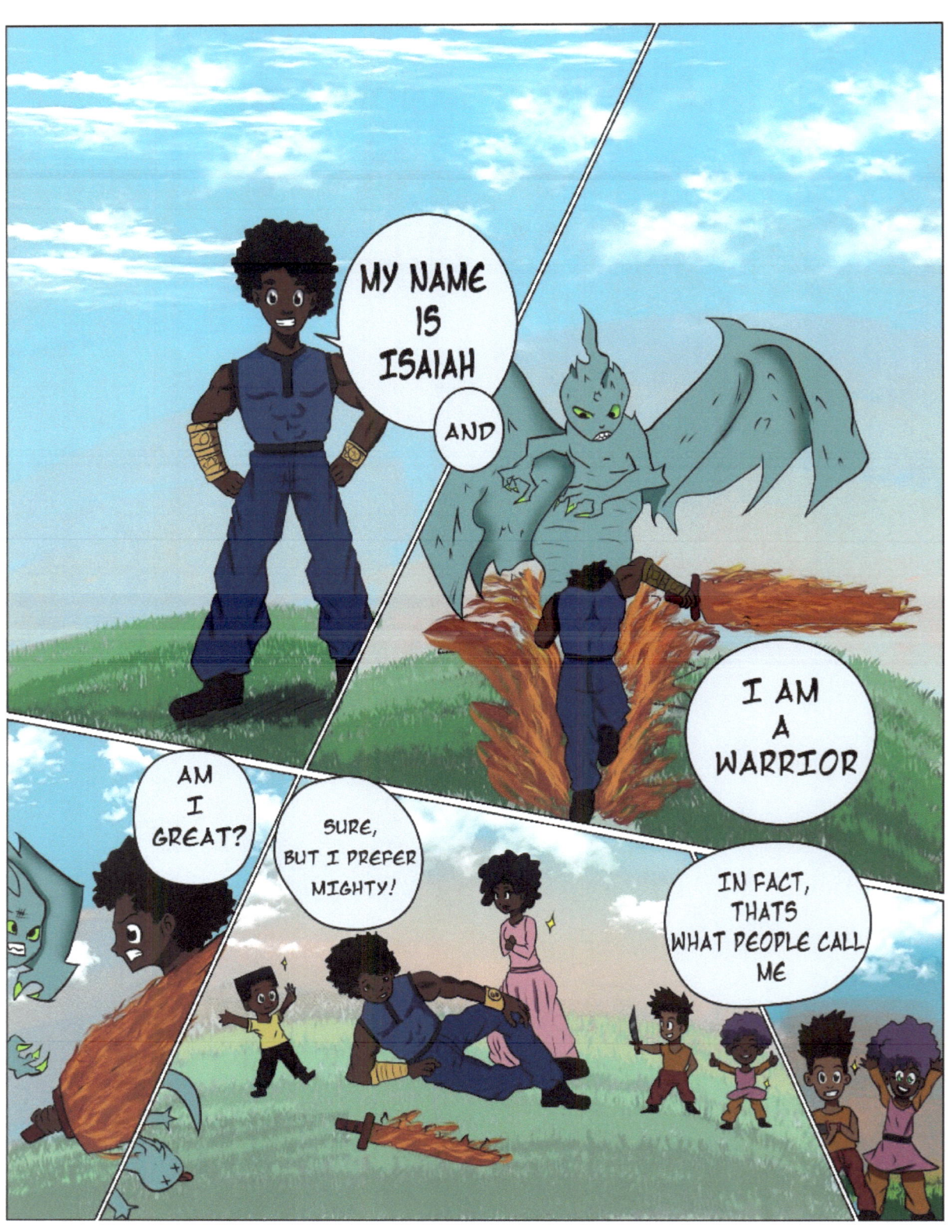

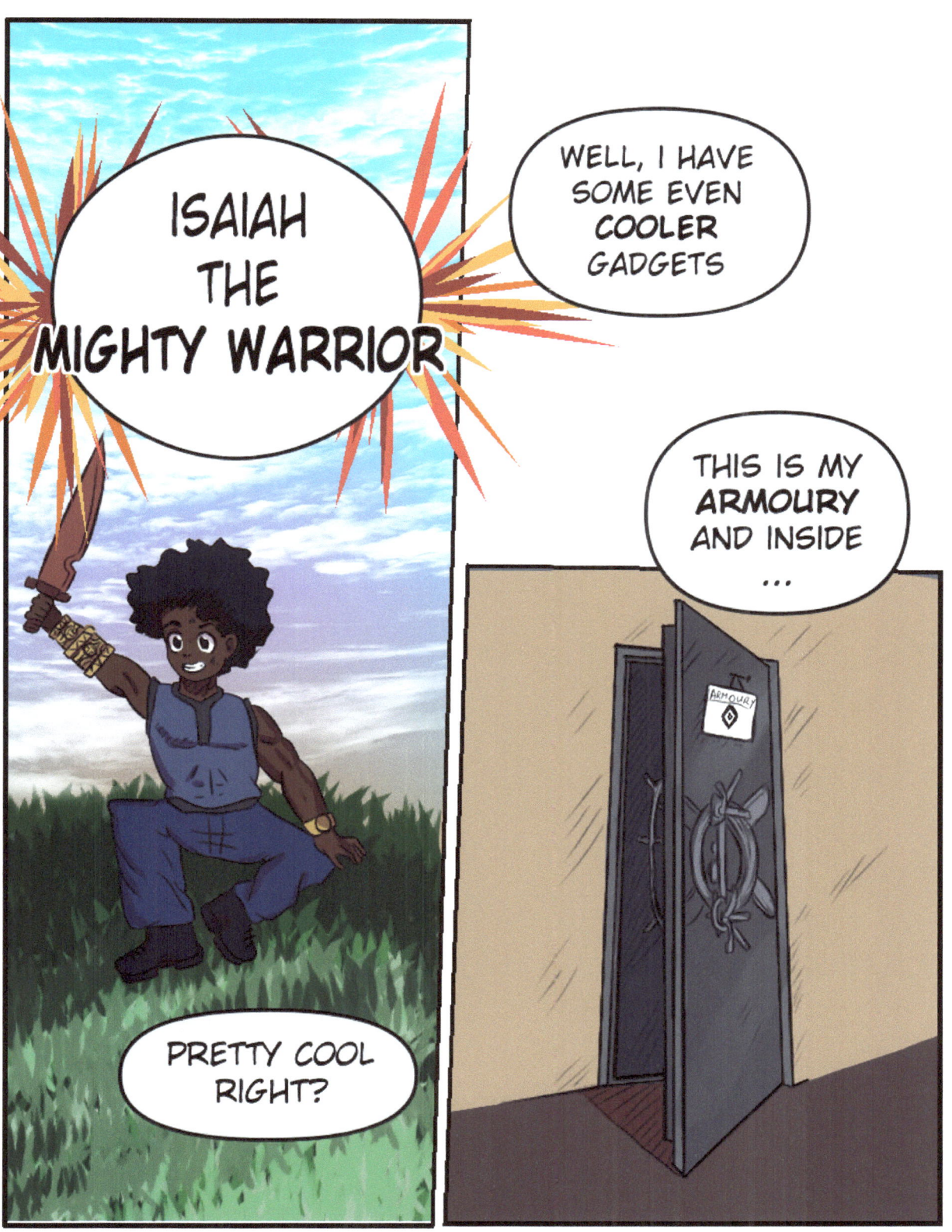

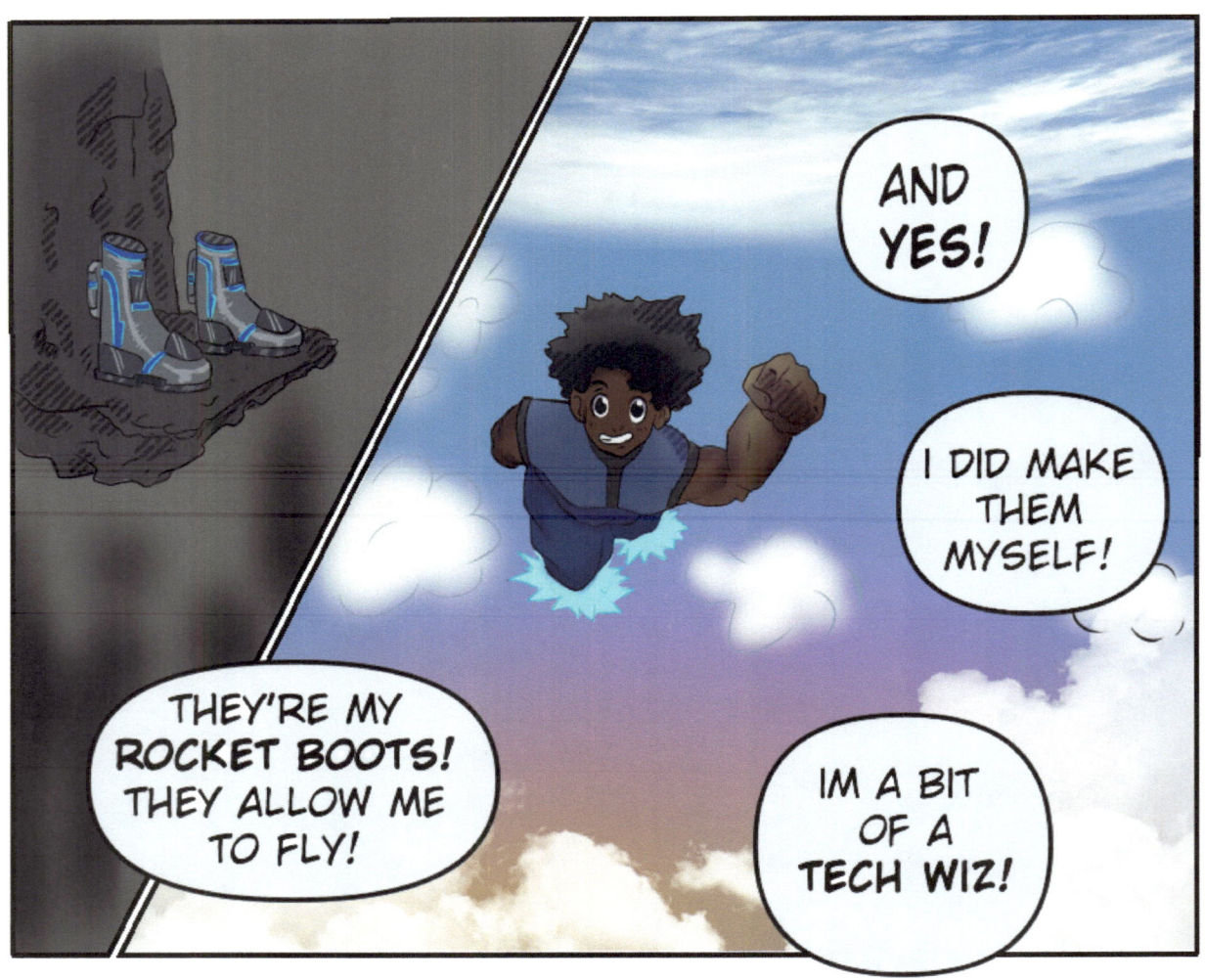

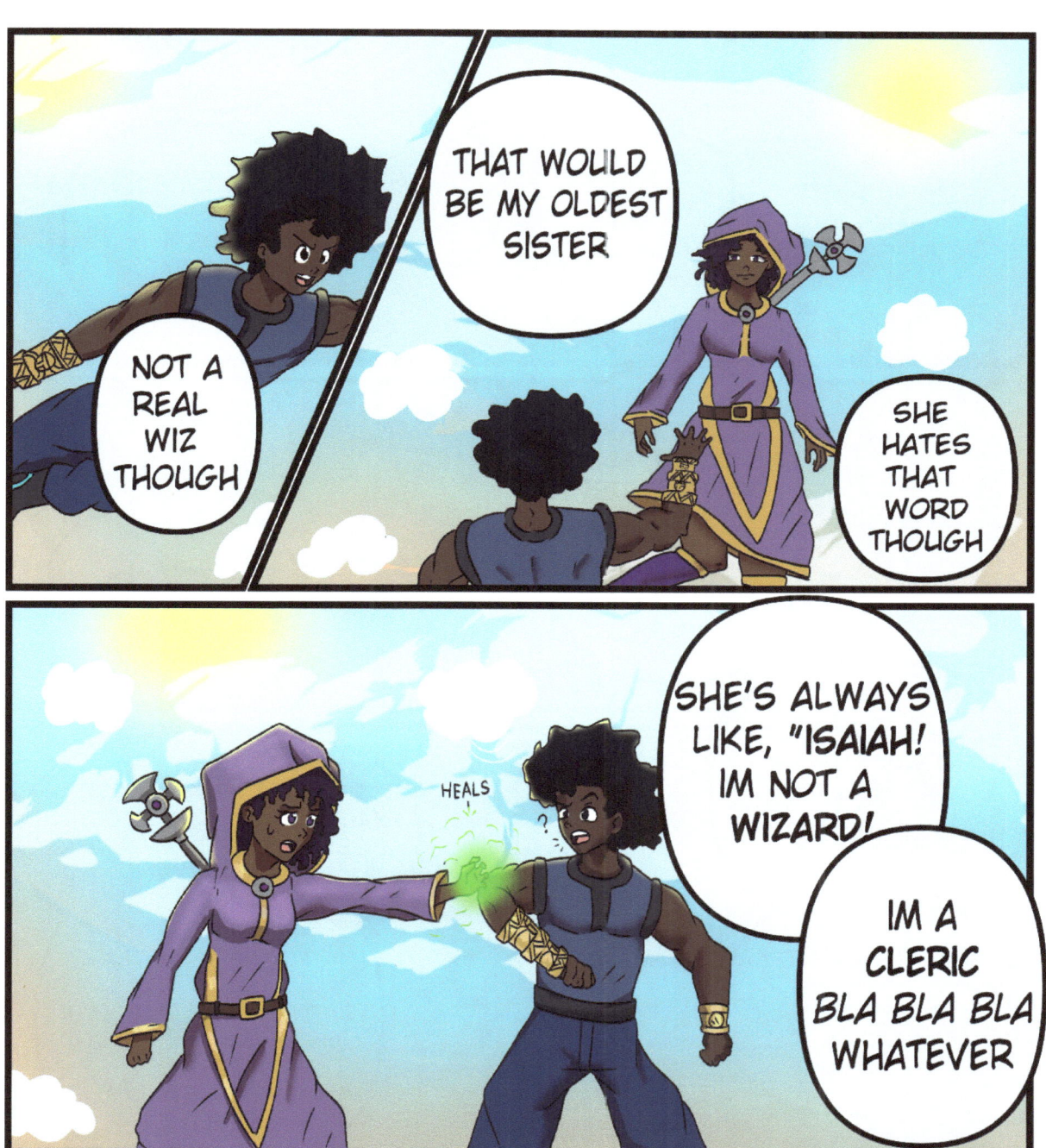

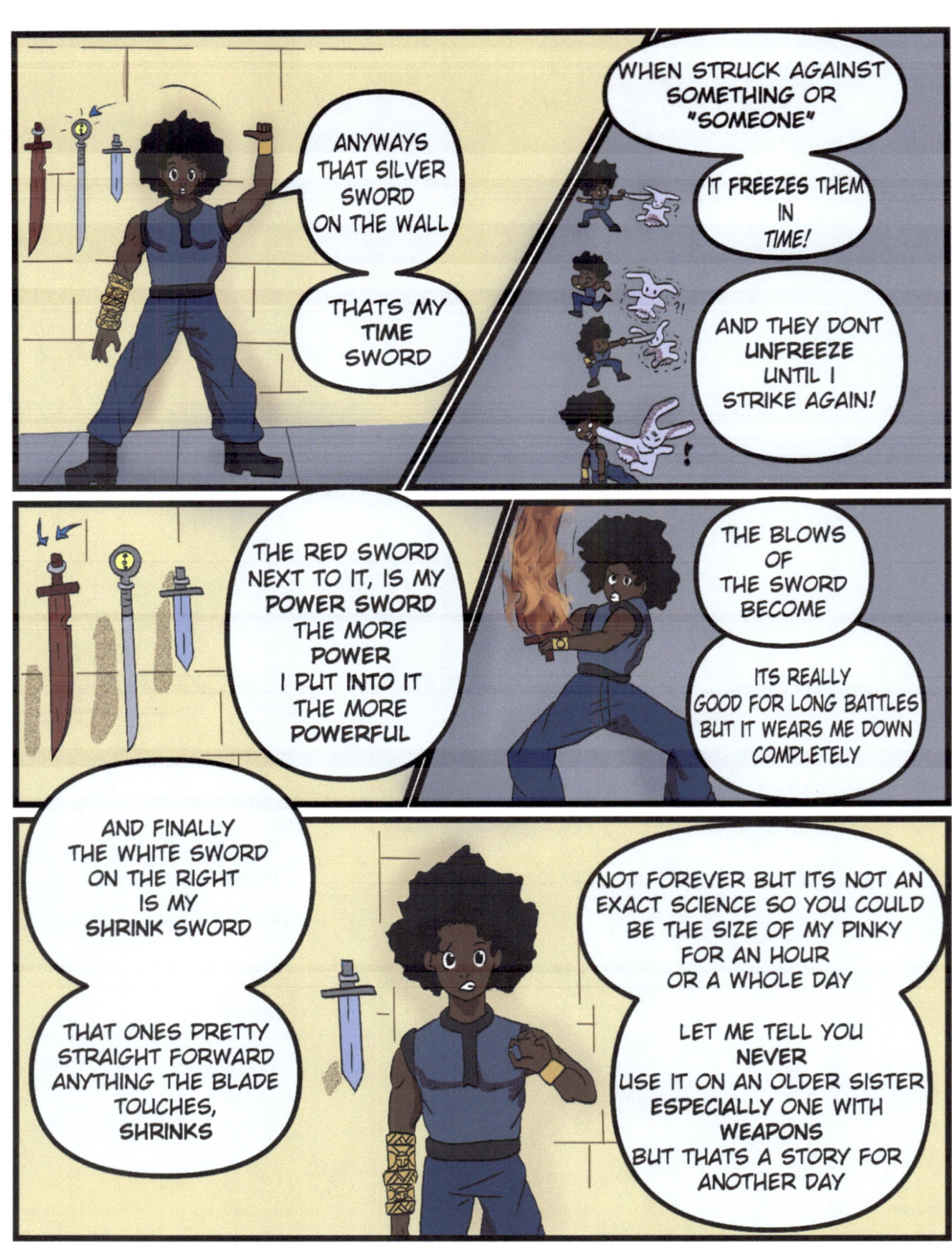

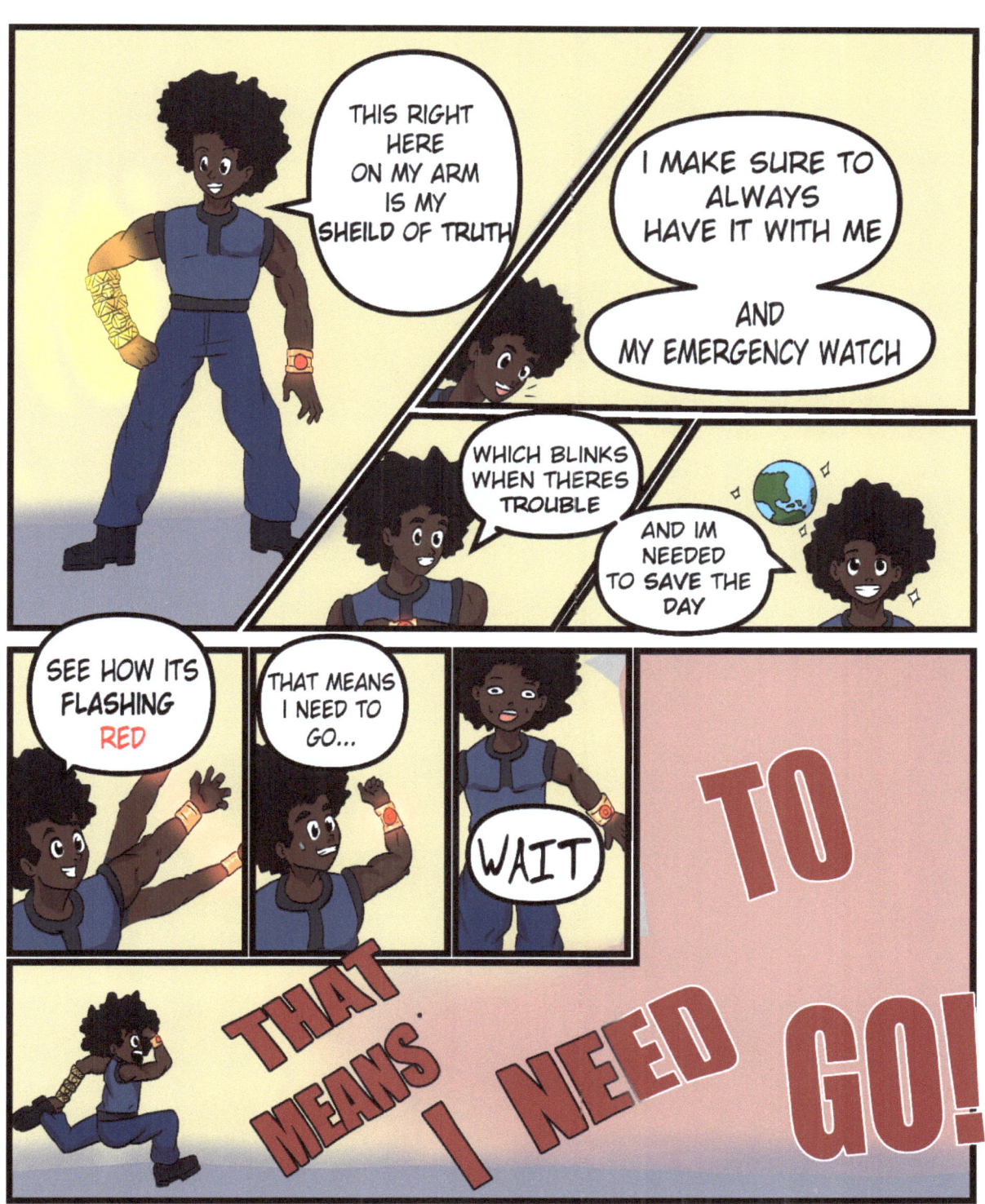

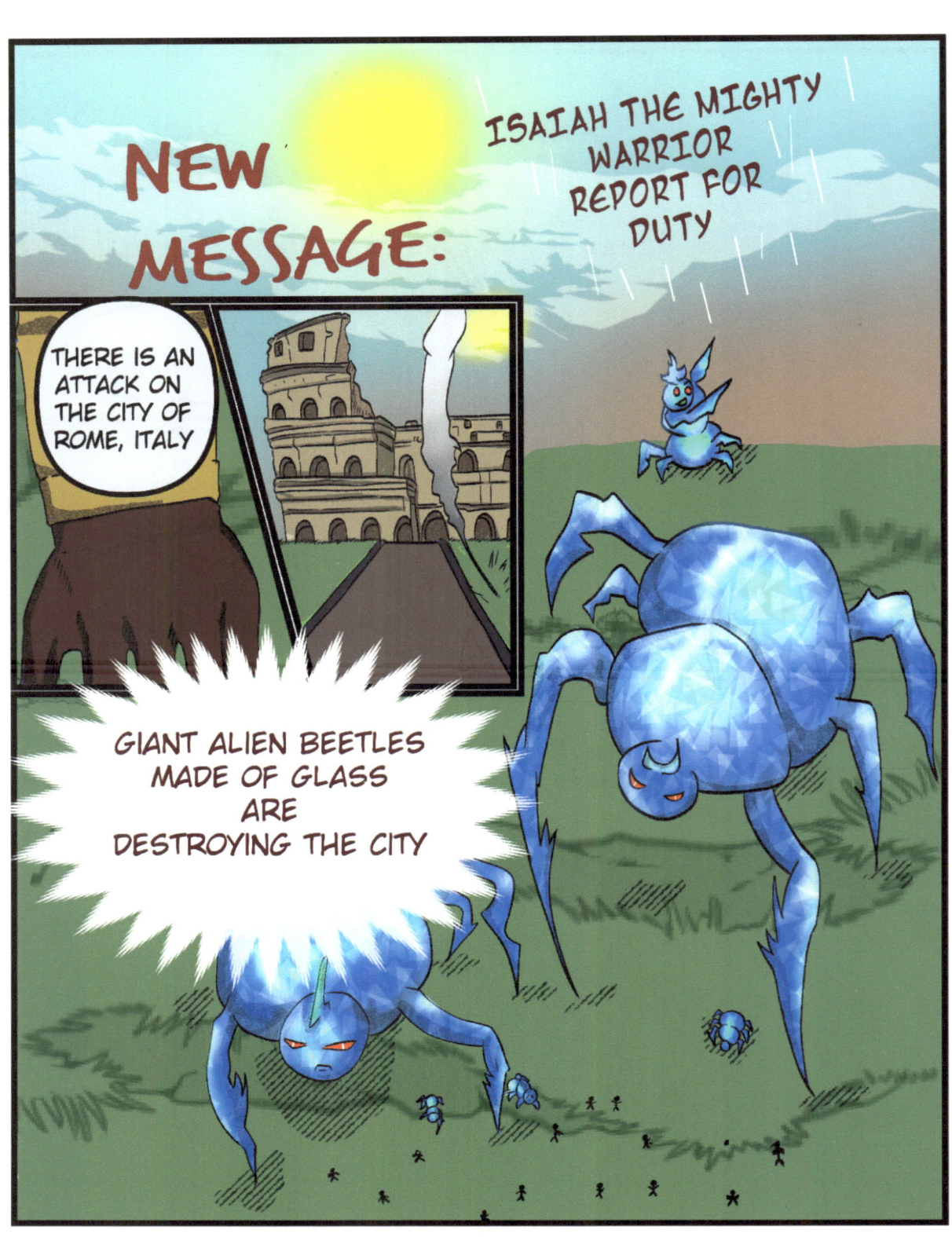

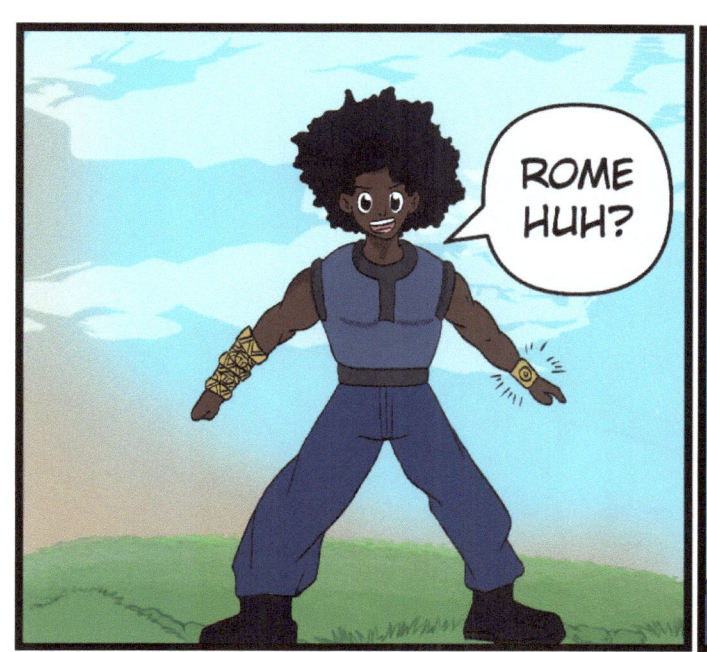

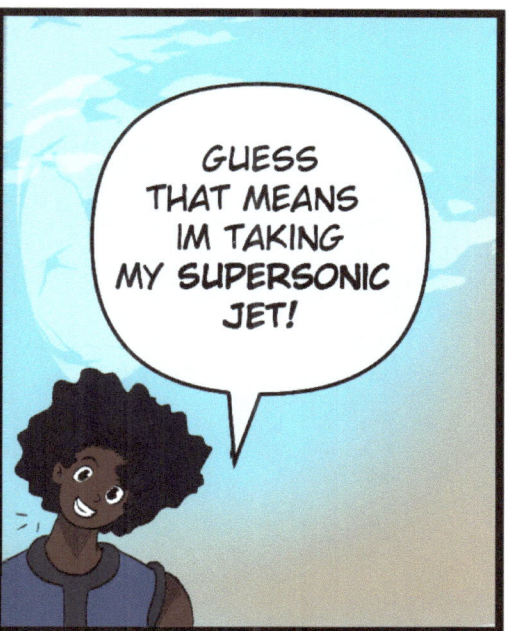

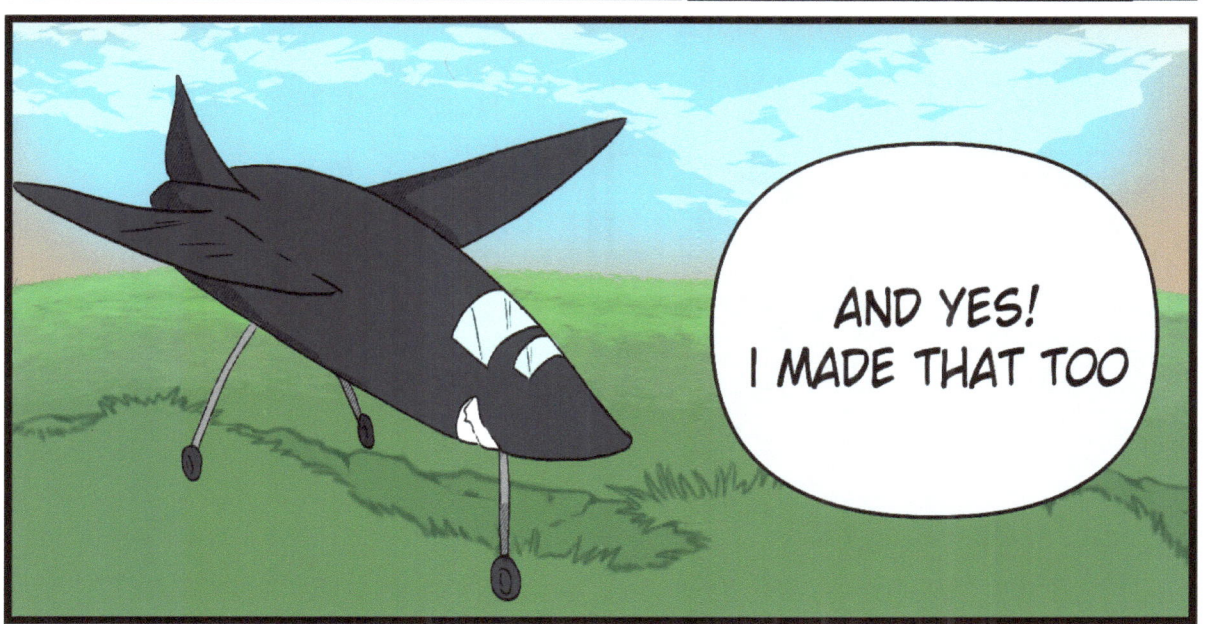

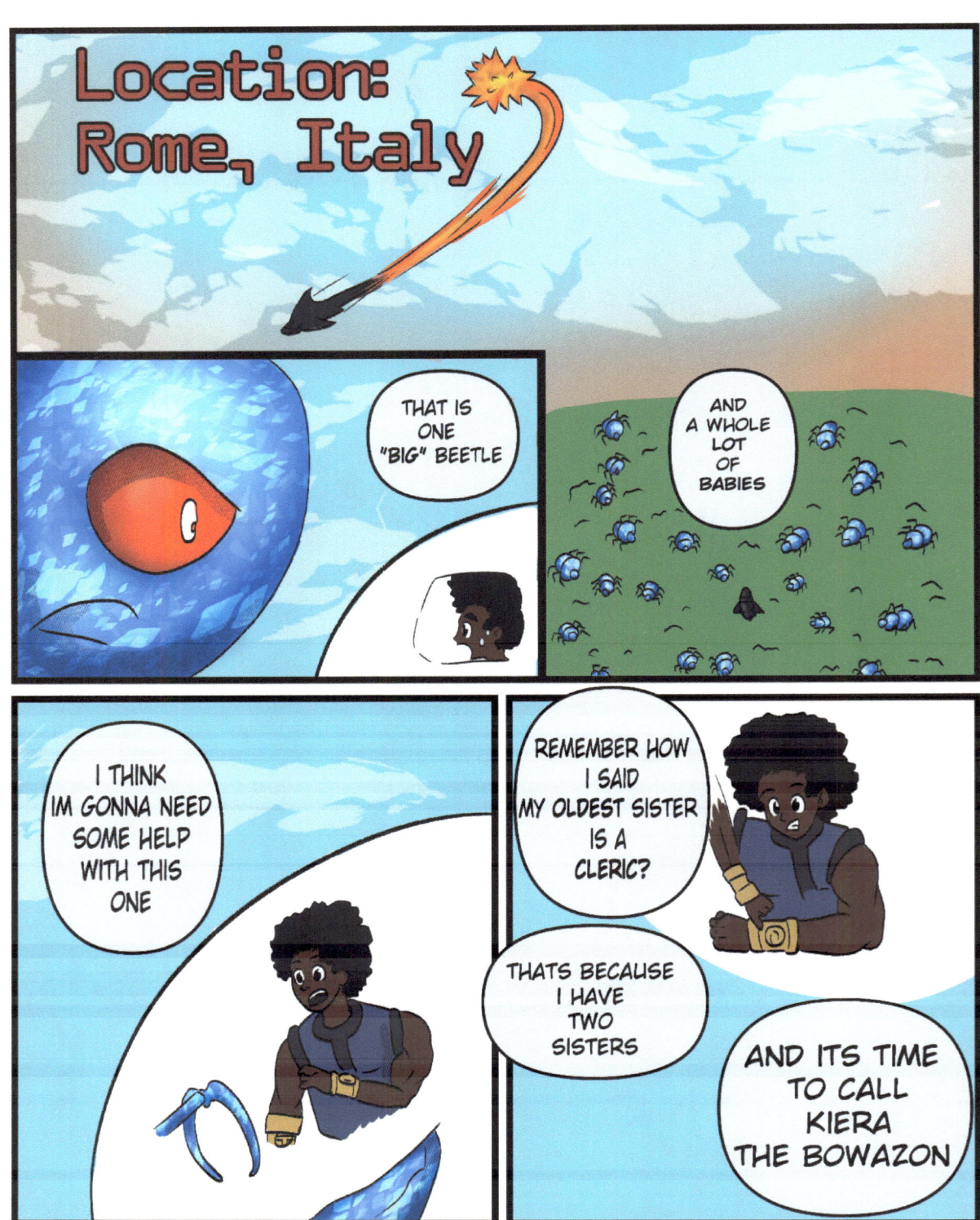

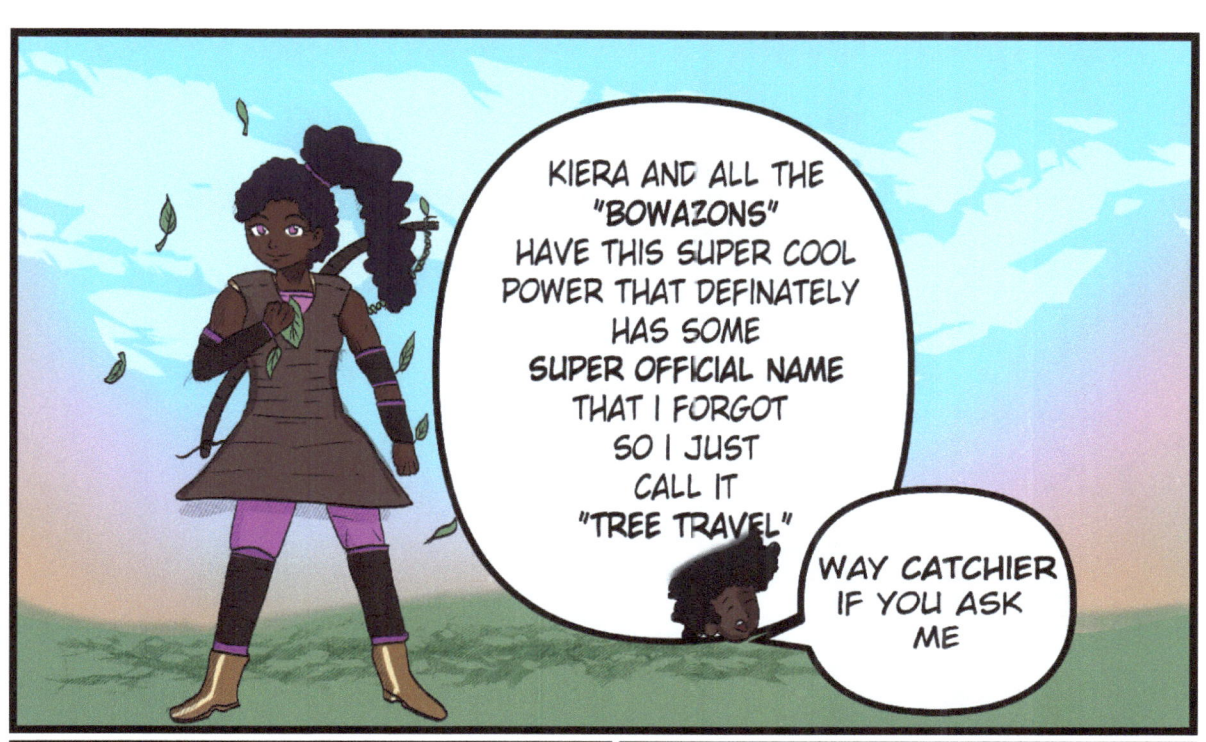

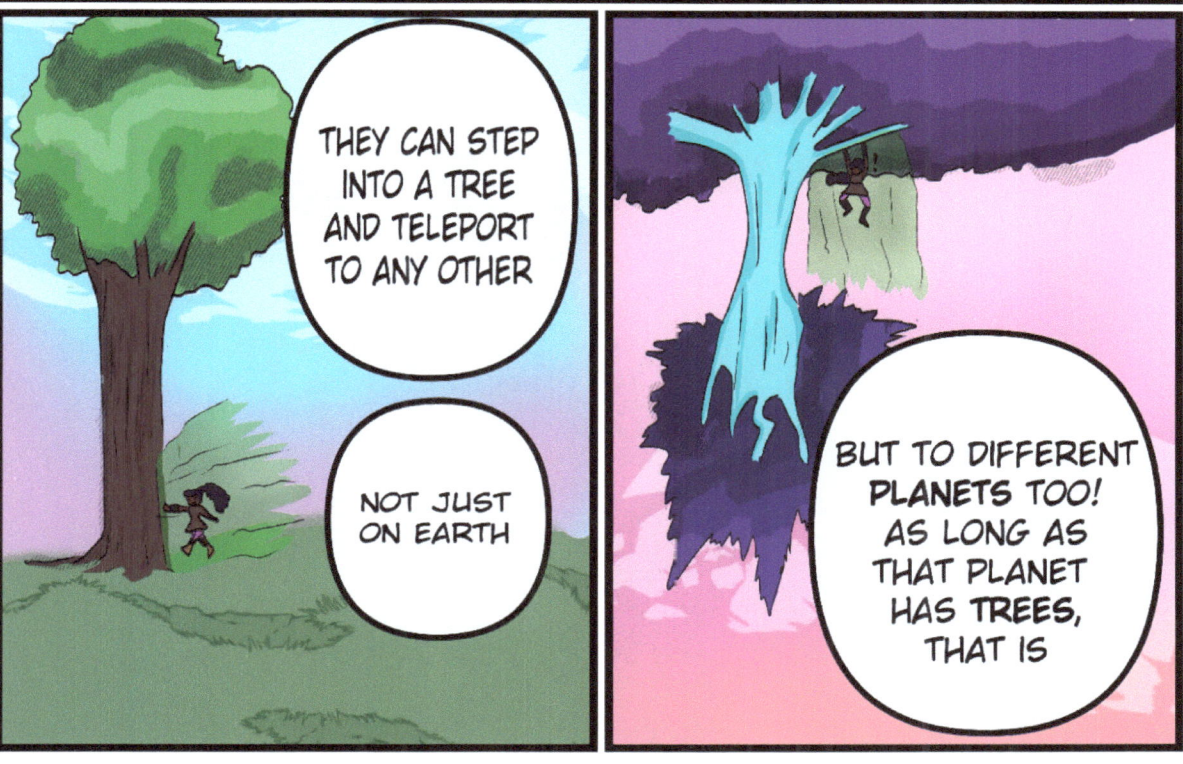

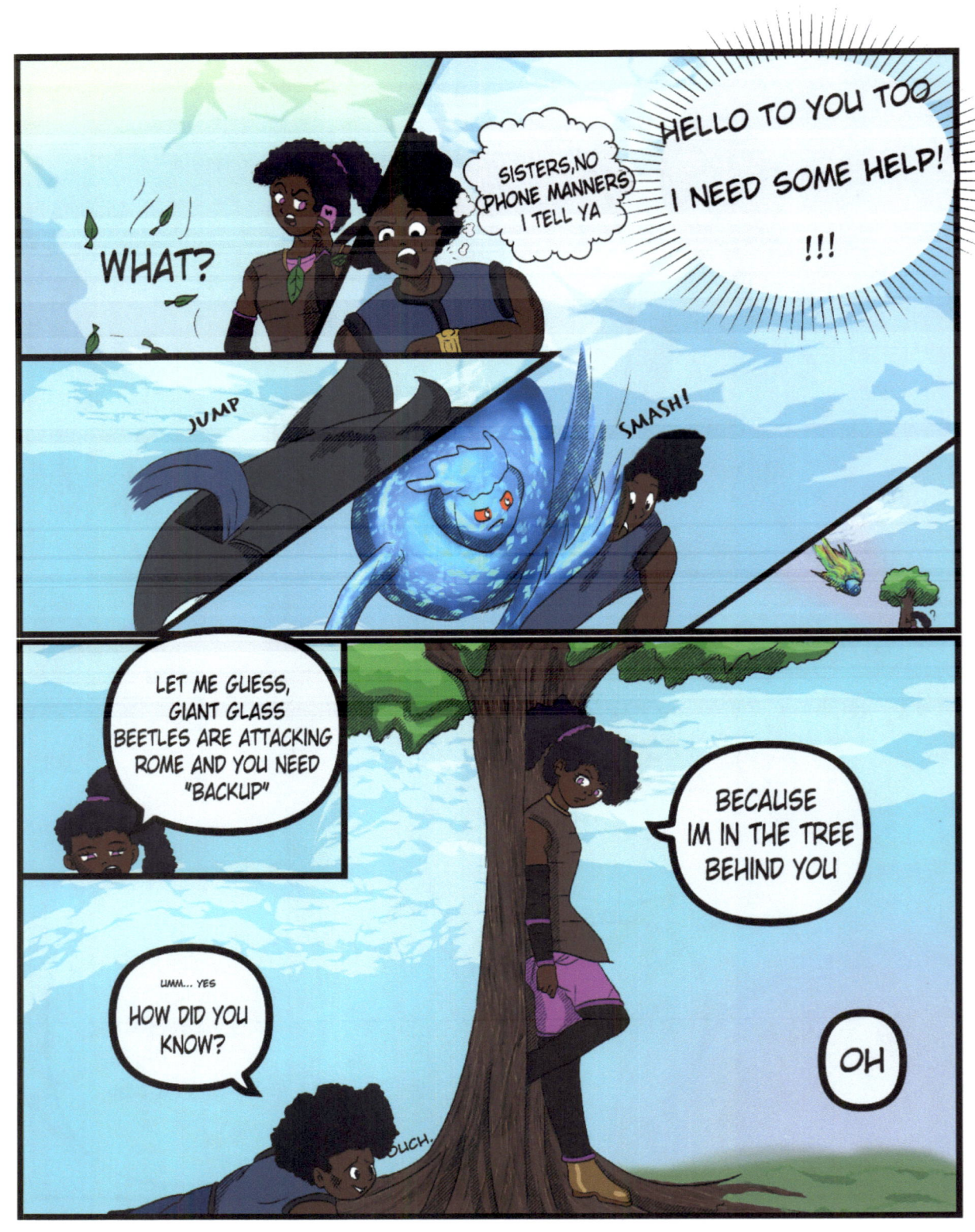

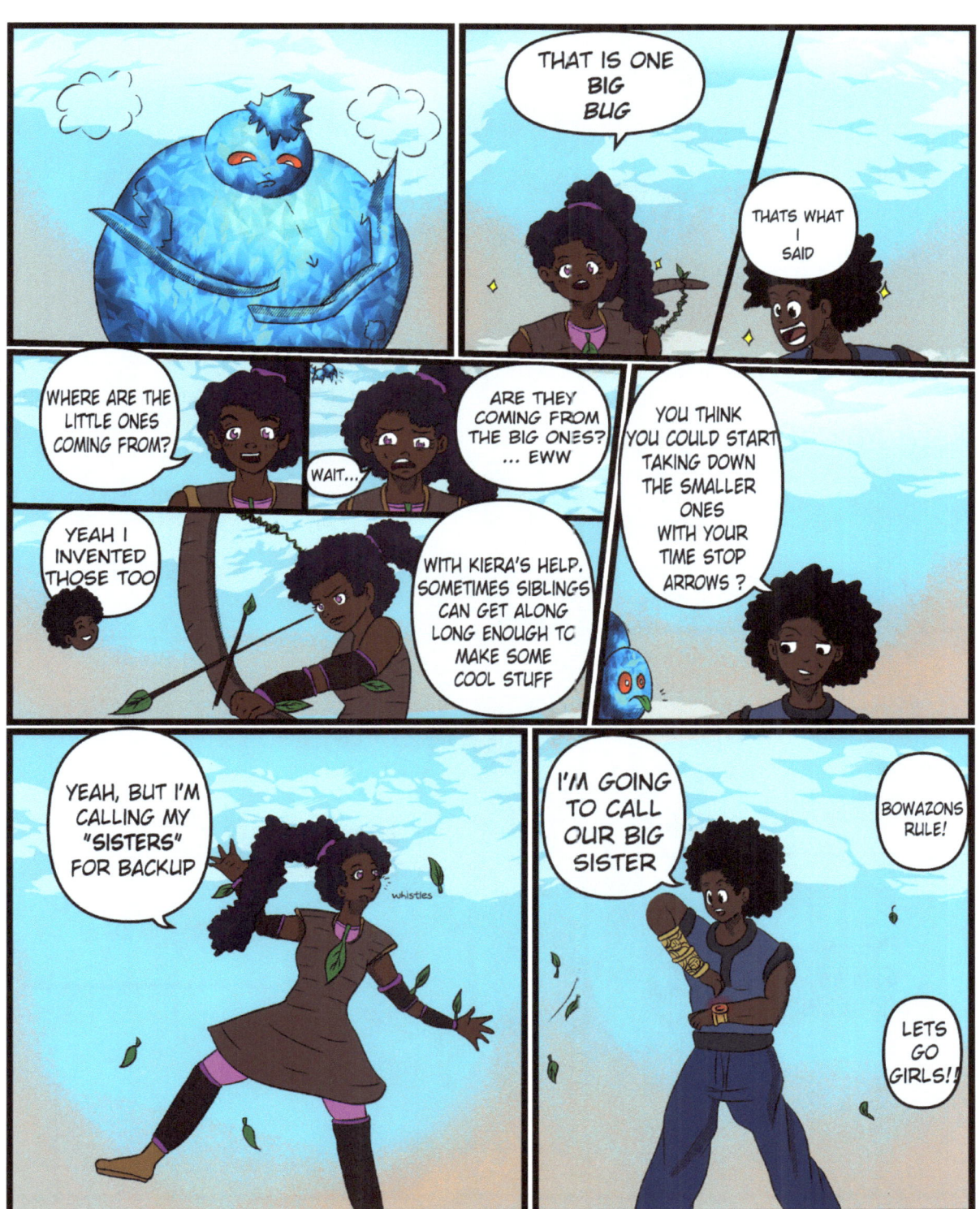

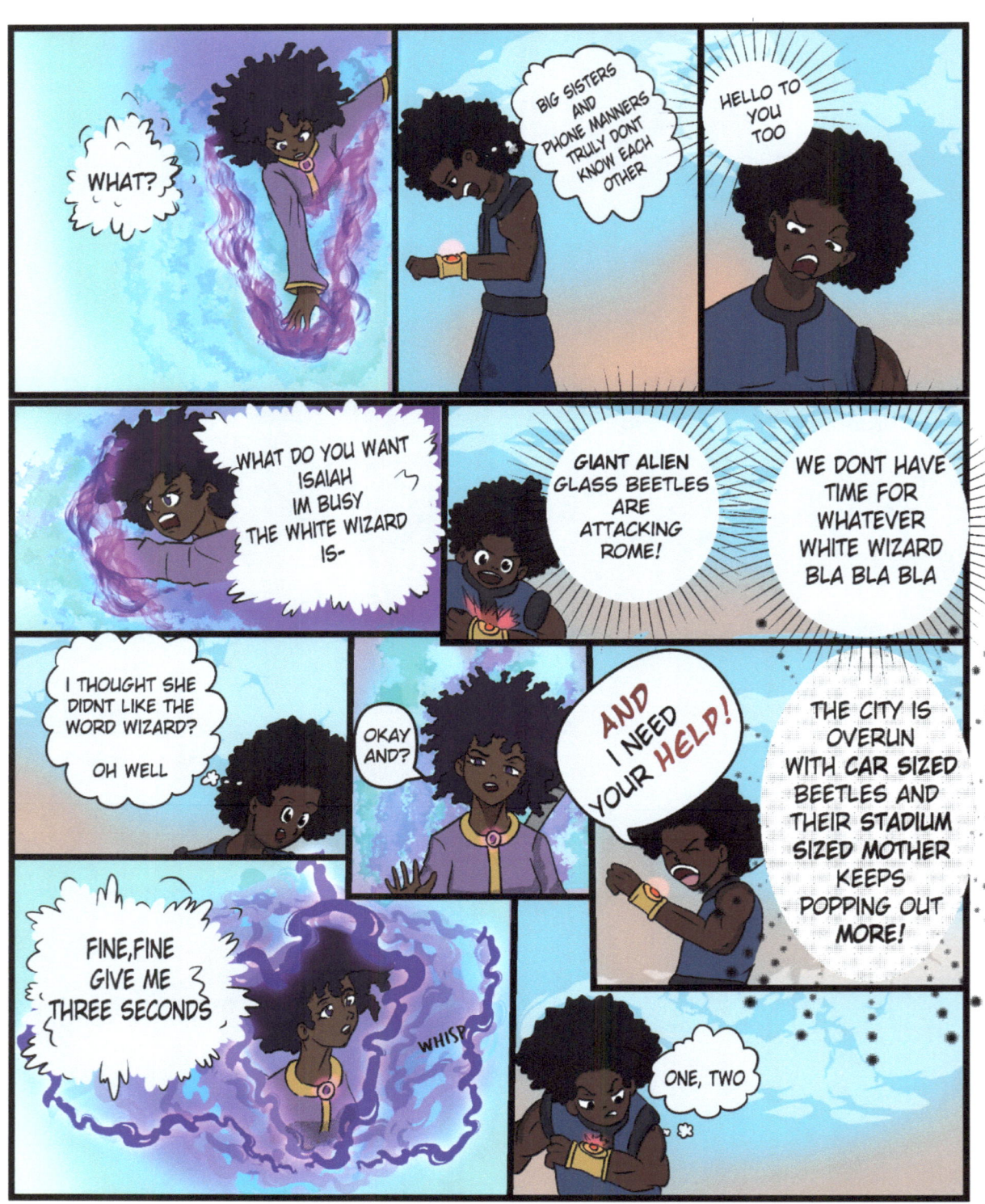

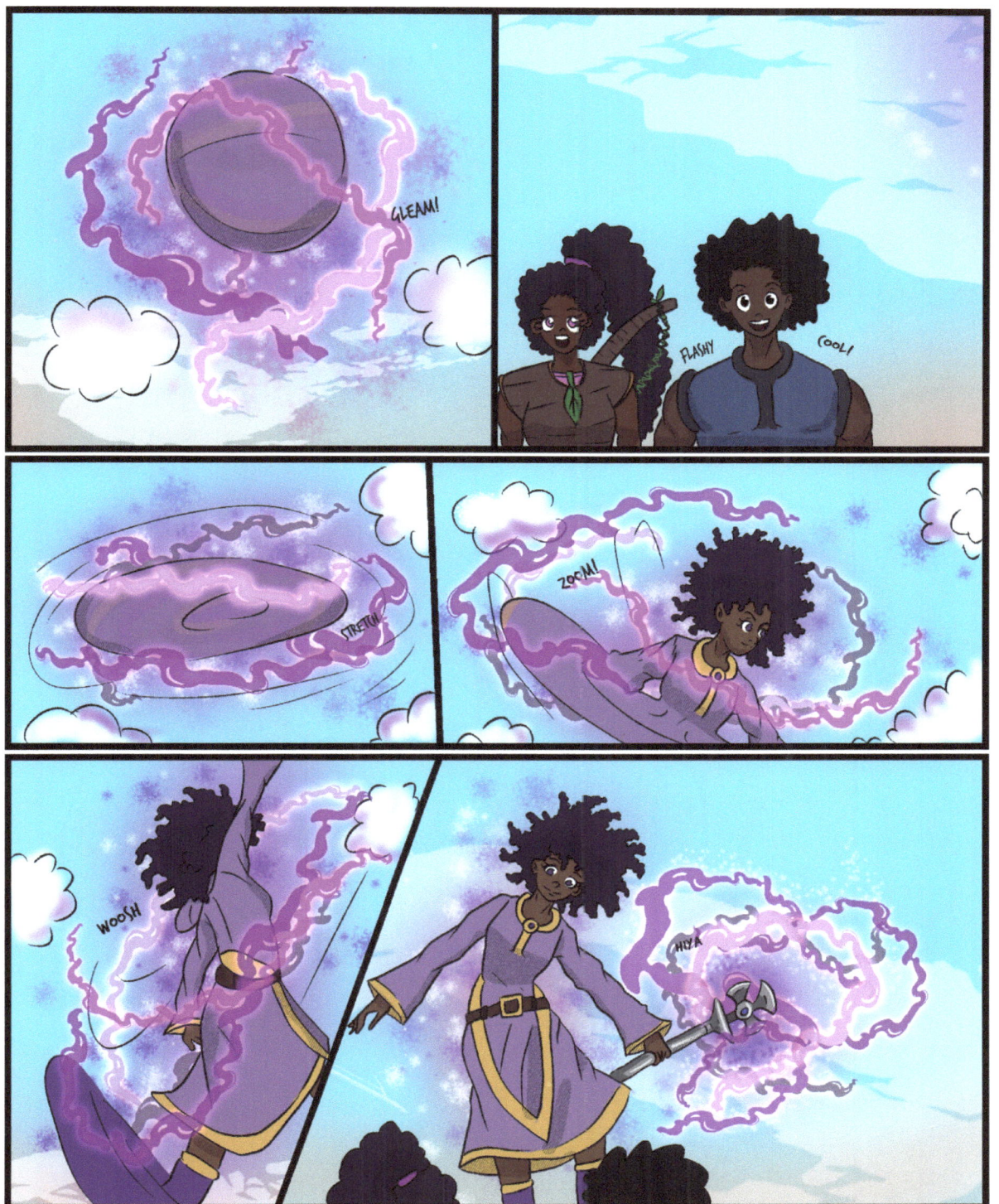

14

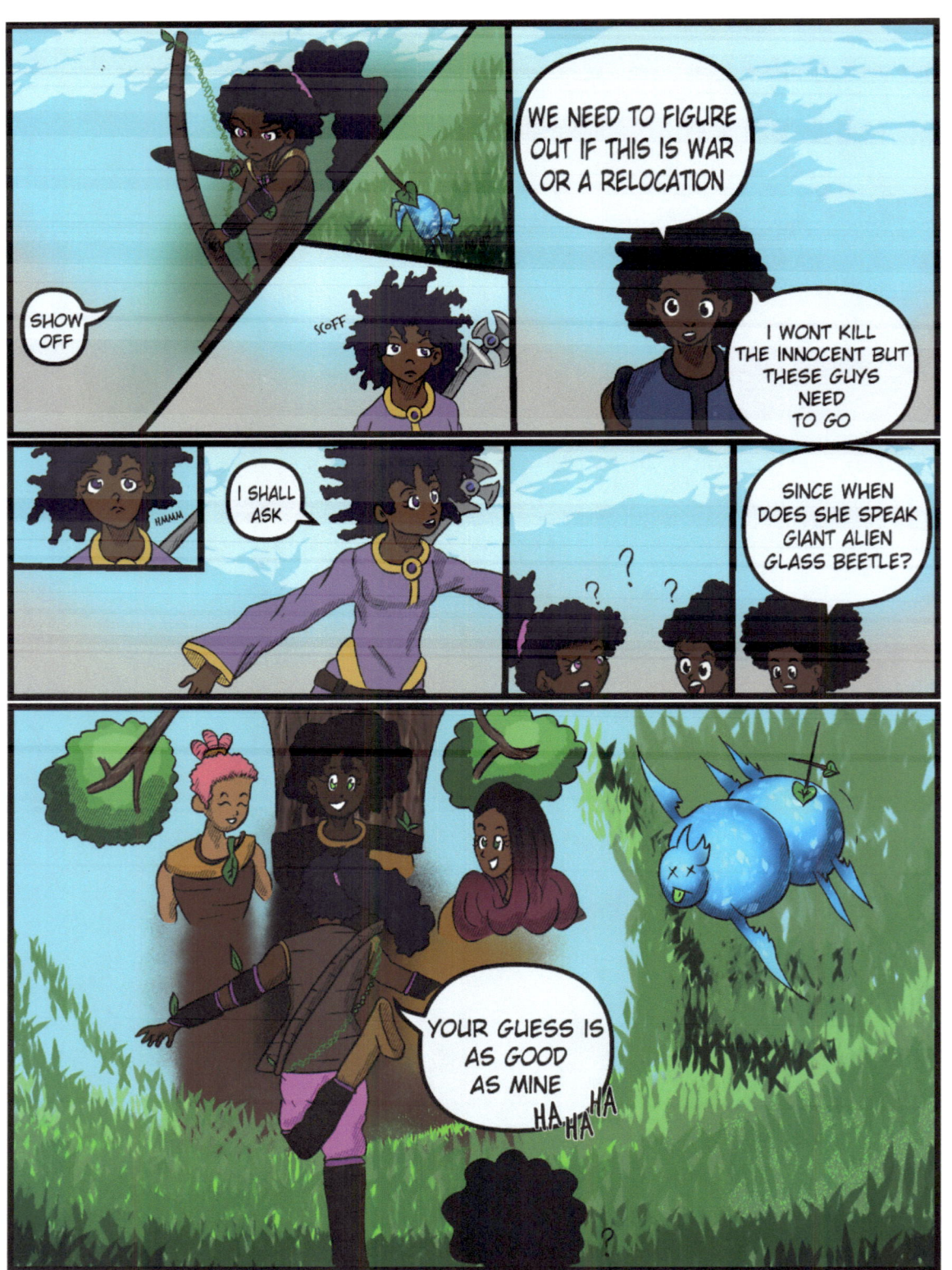

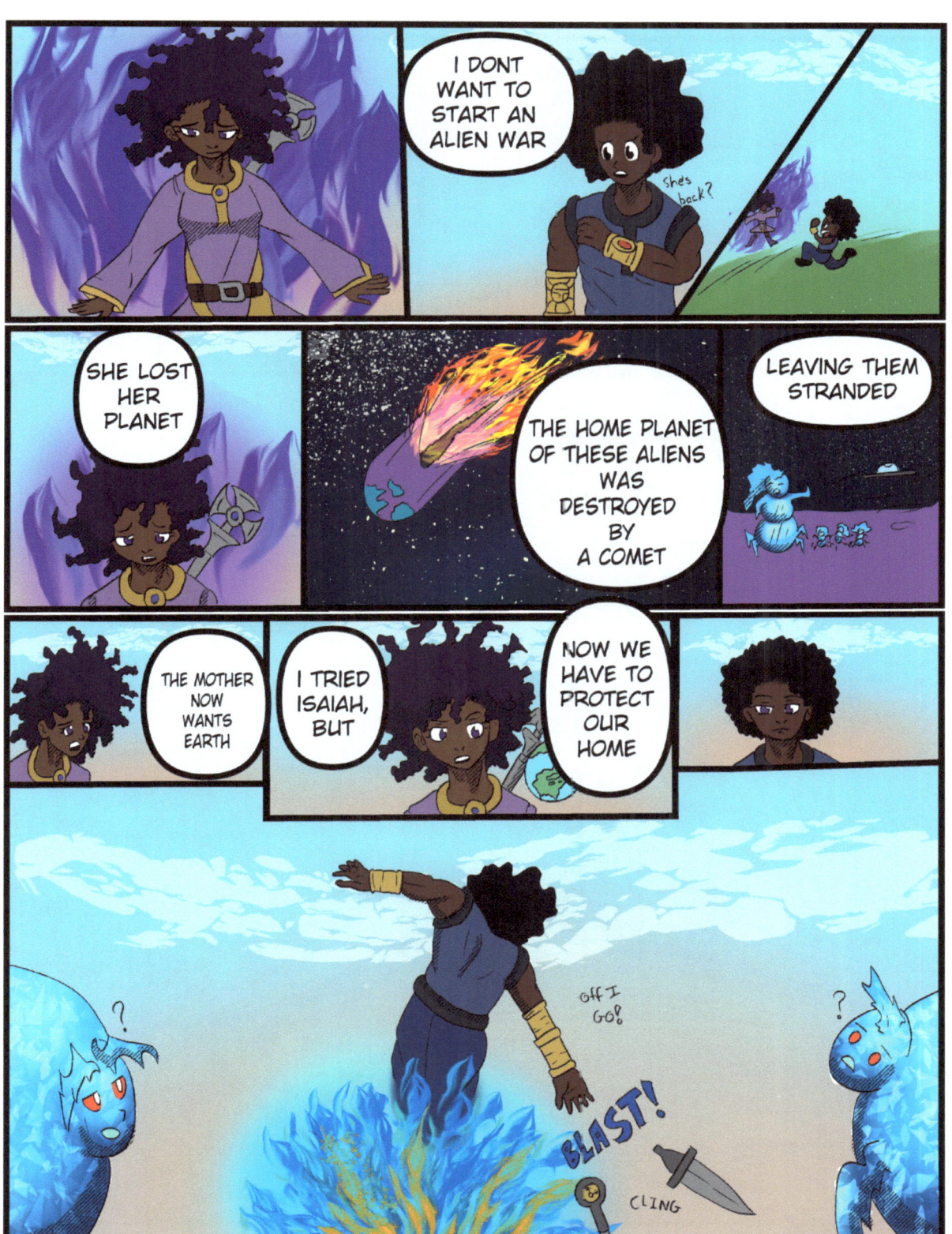

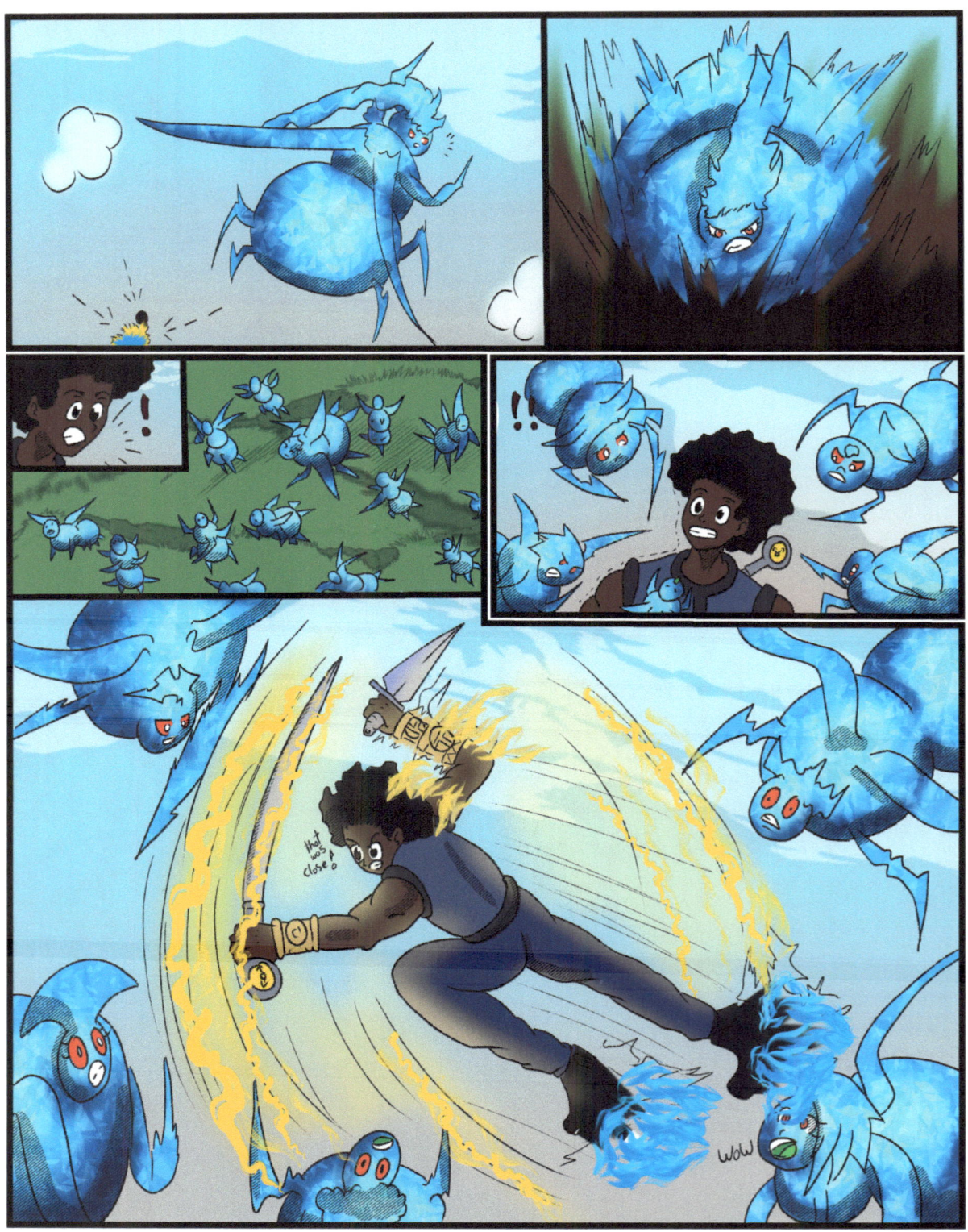

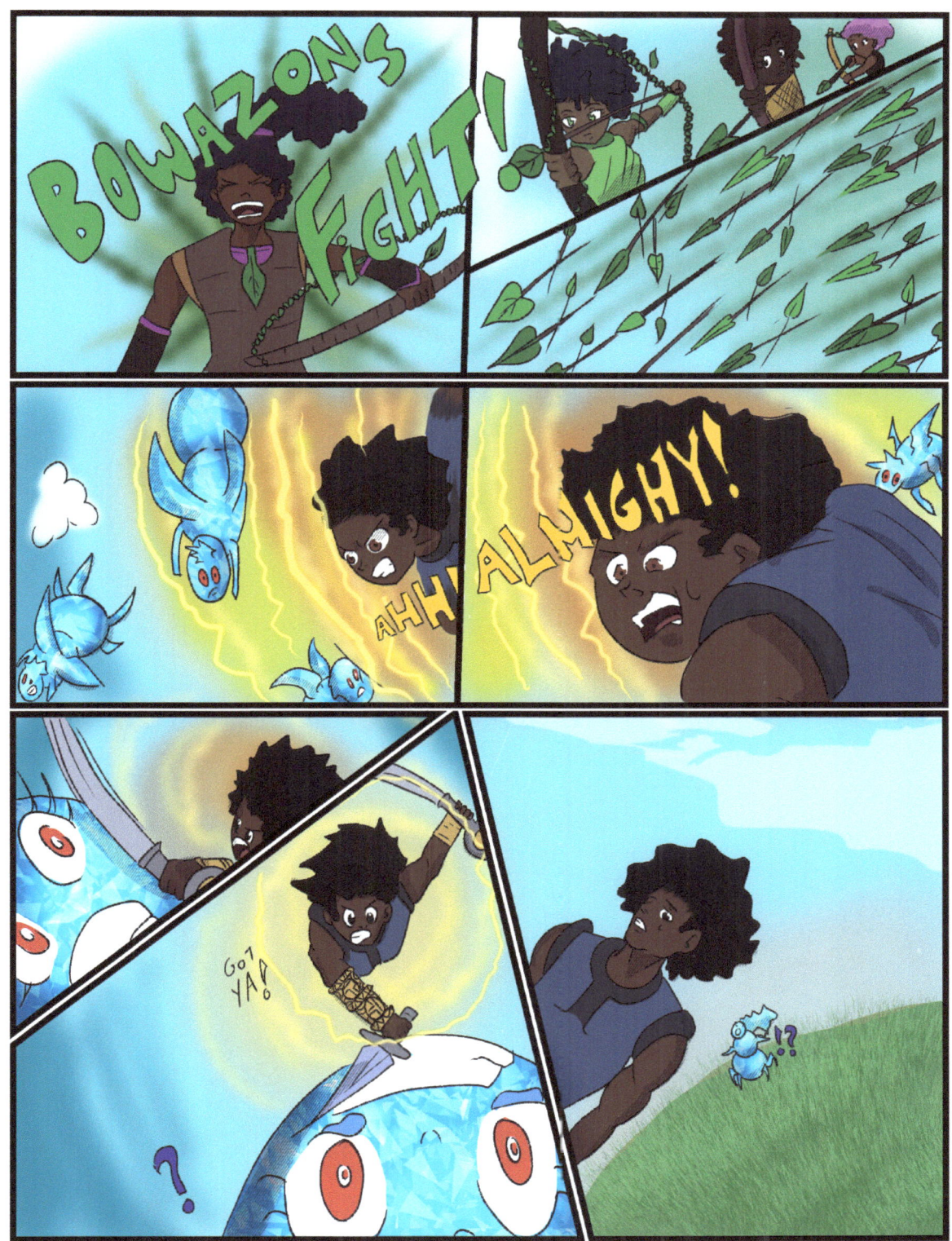

18

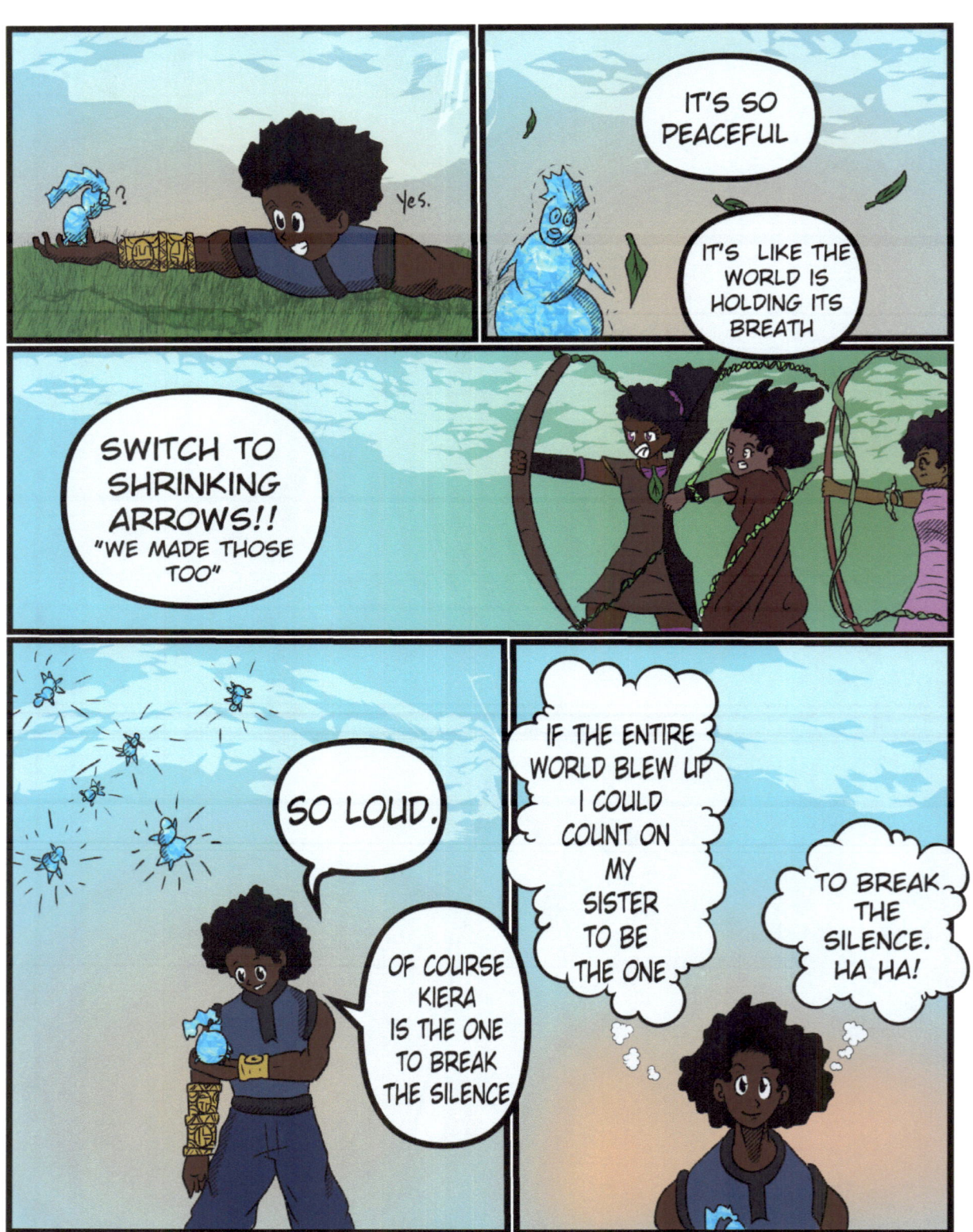

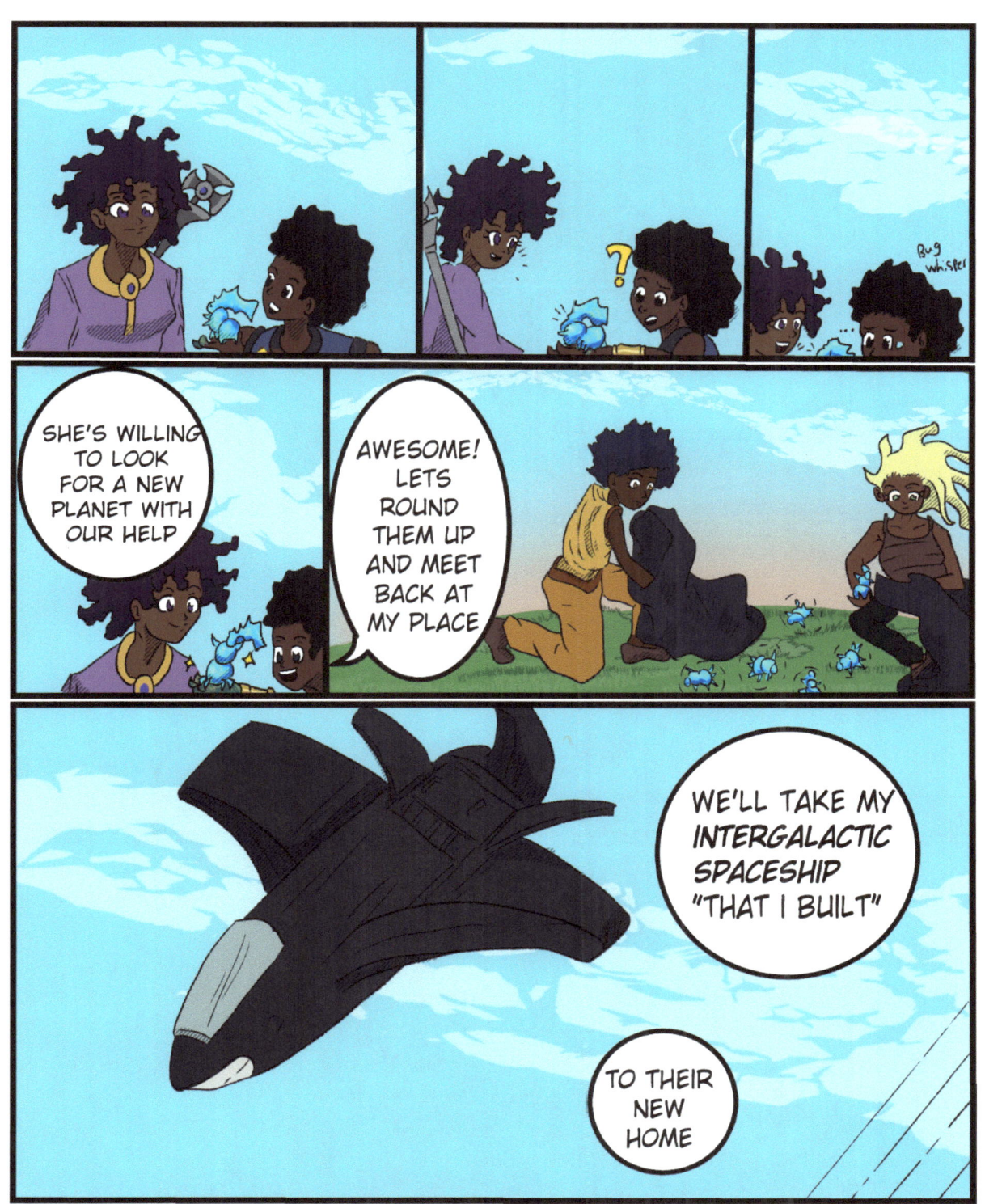

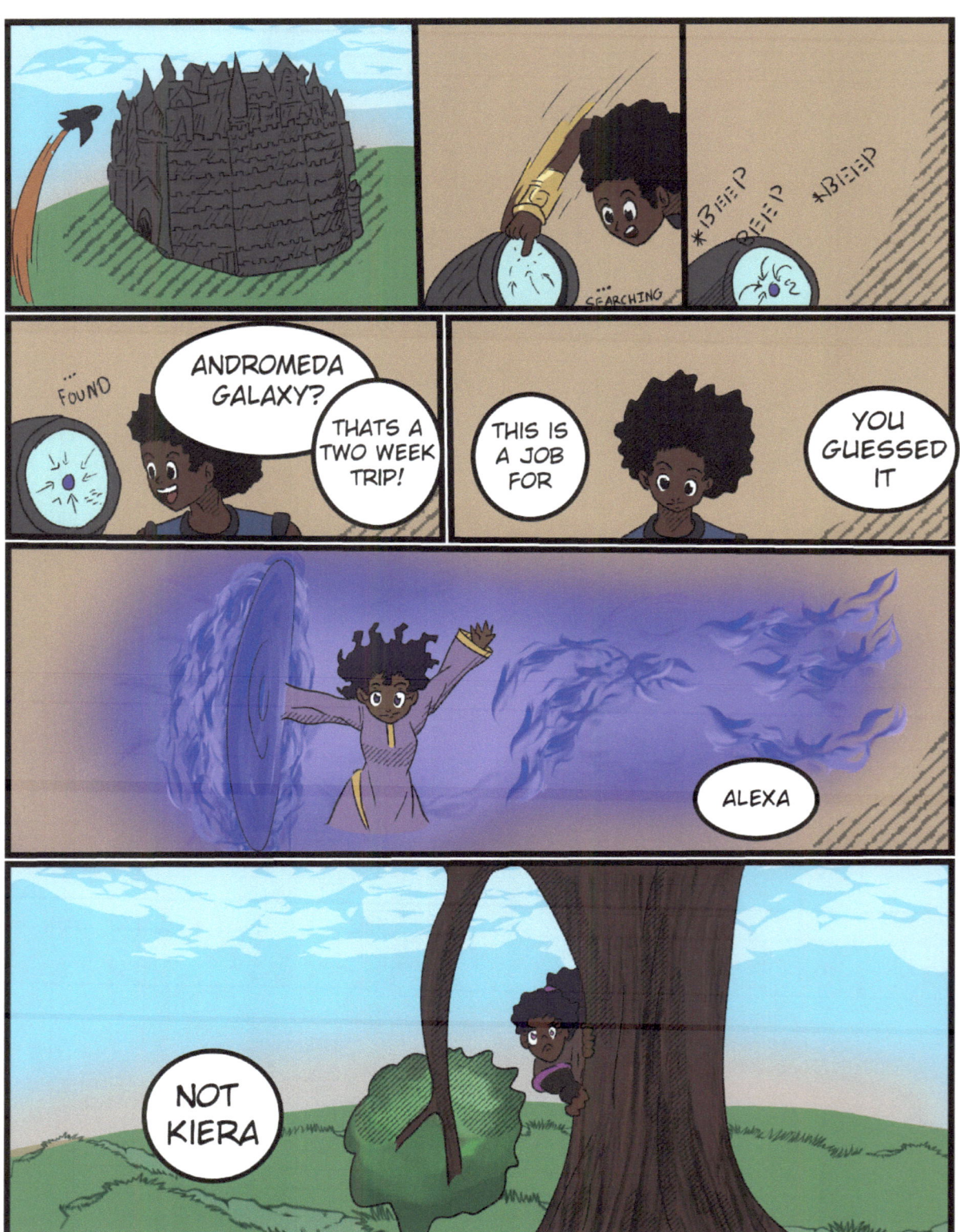

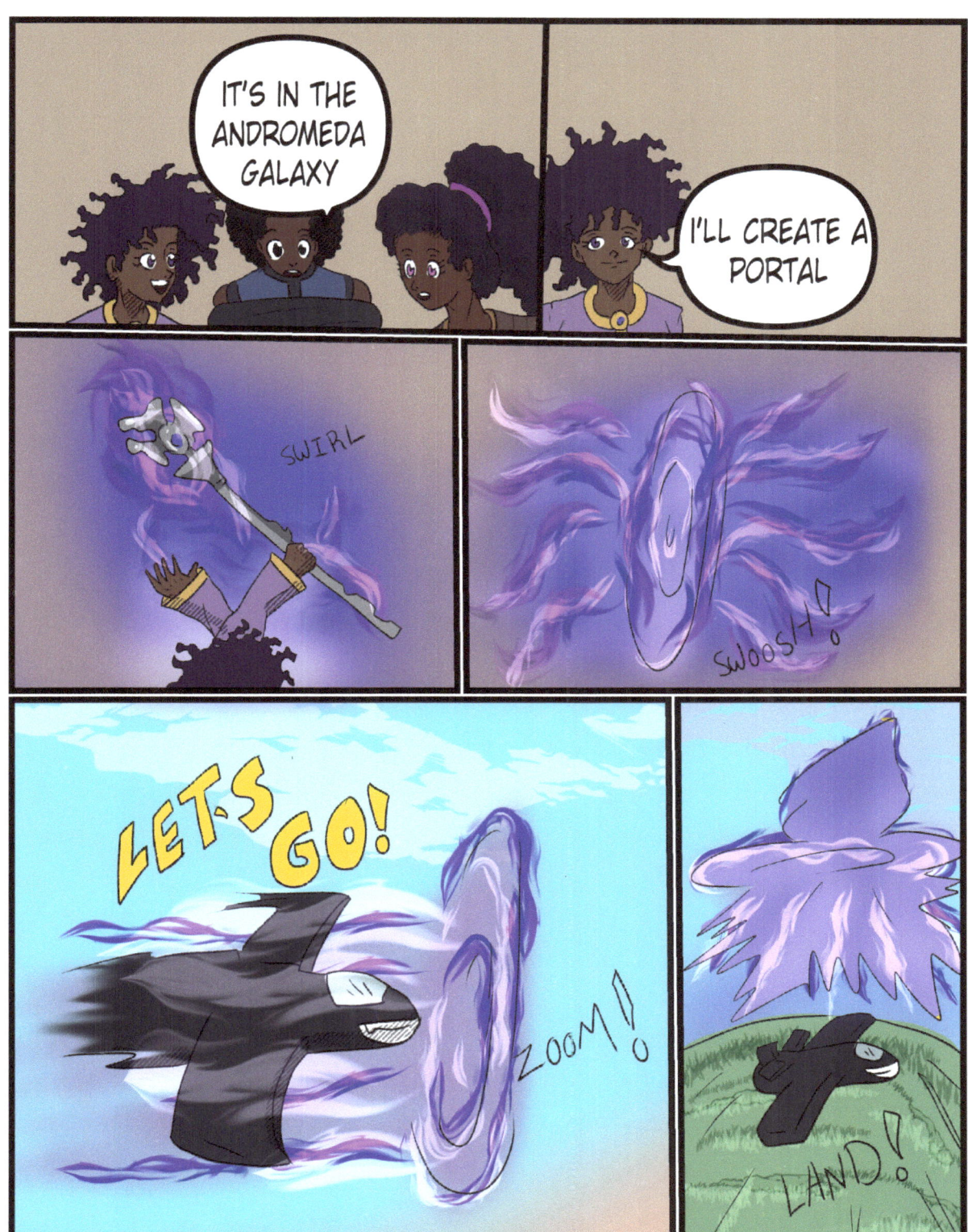

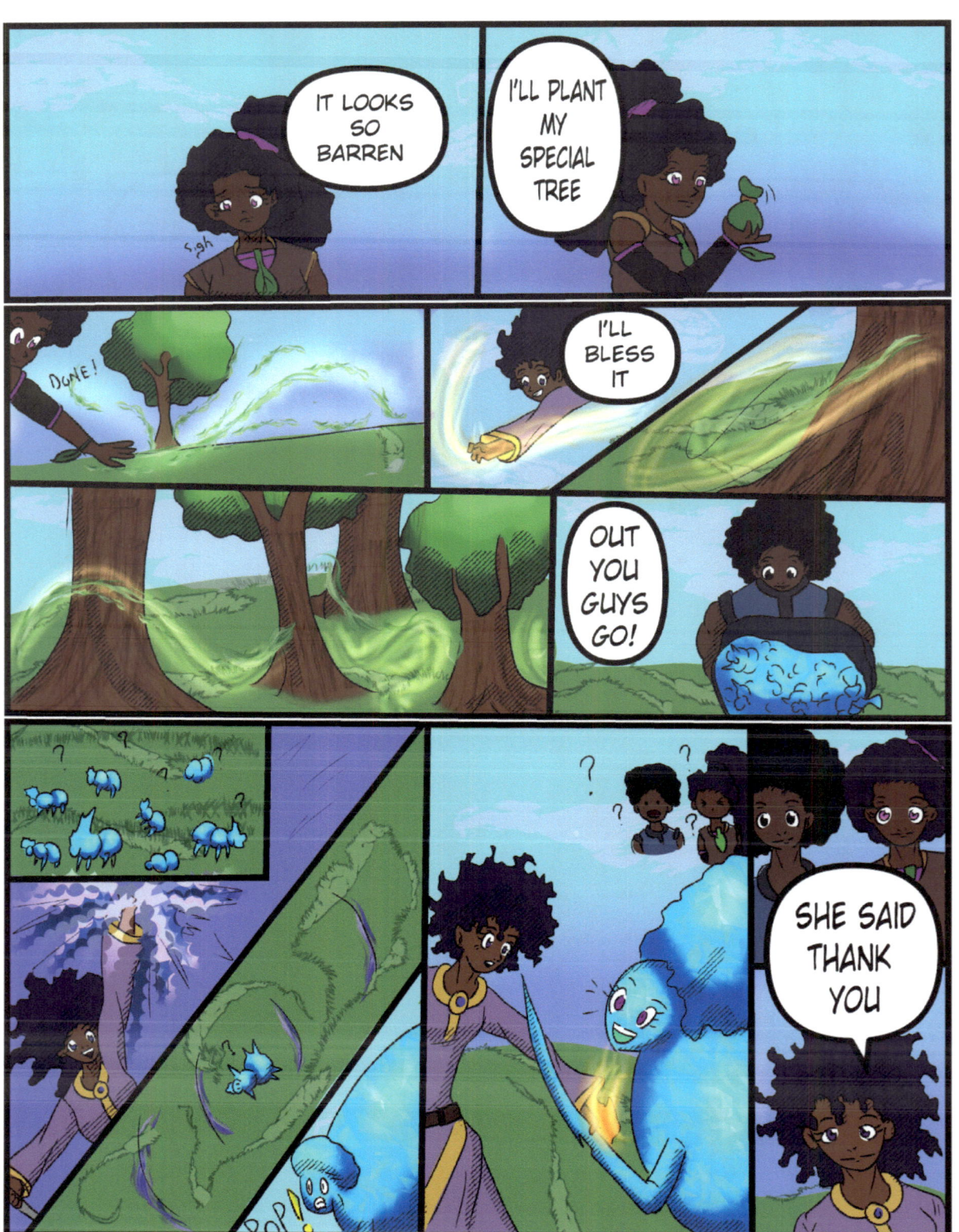

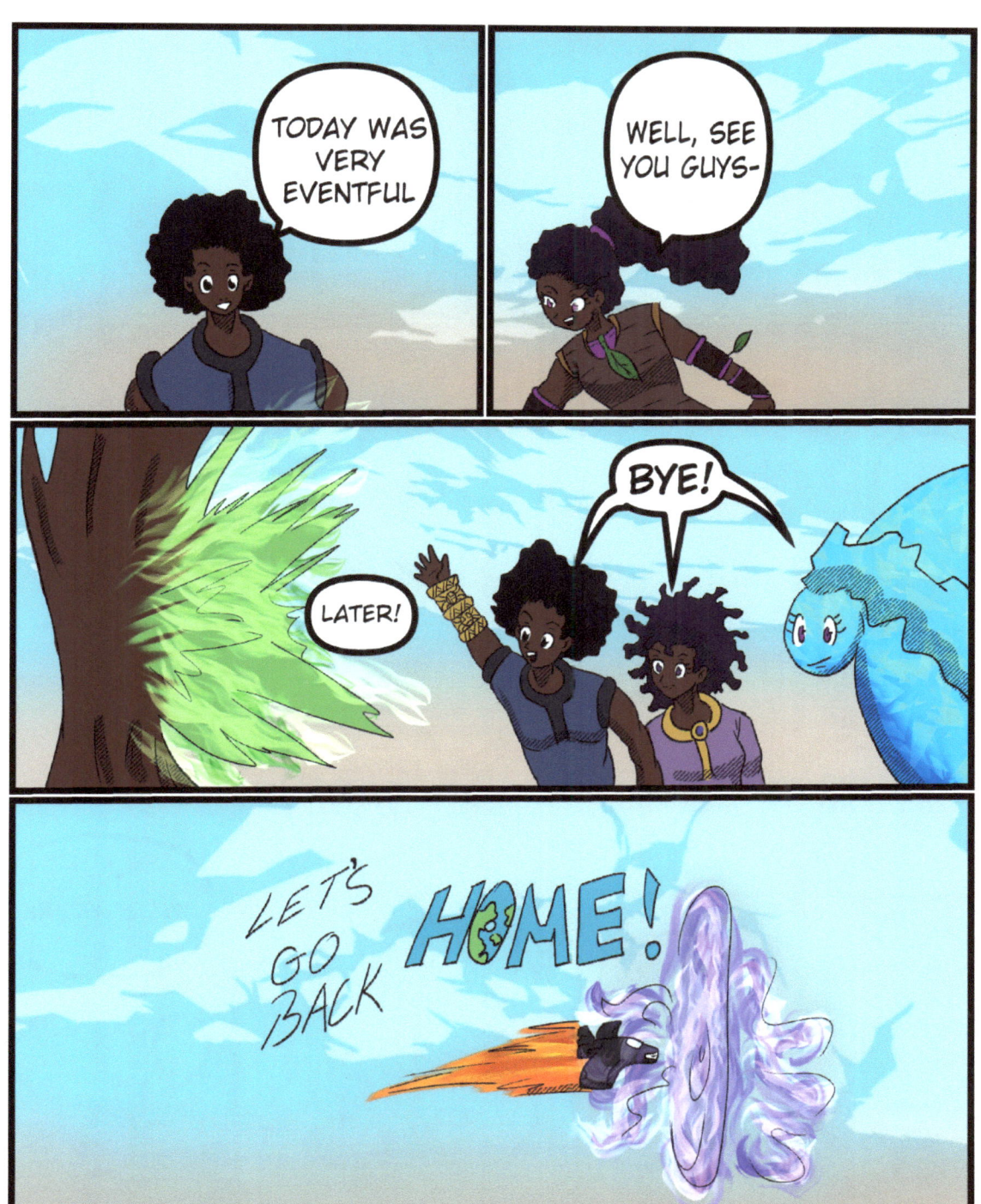

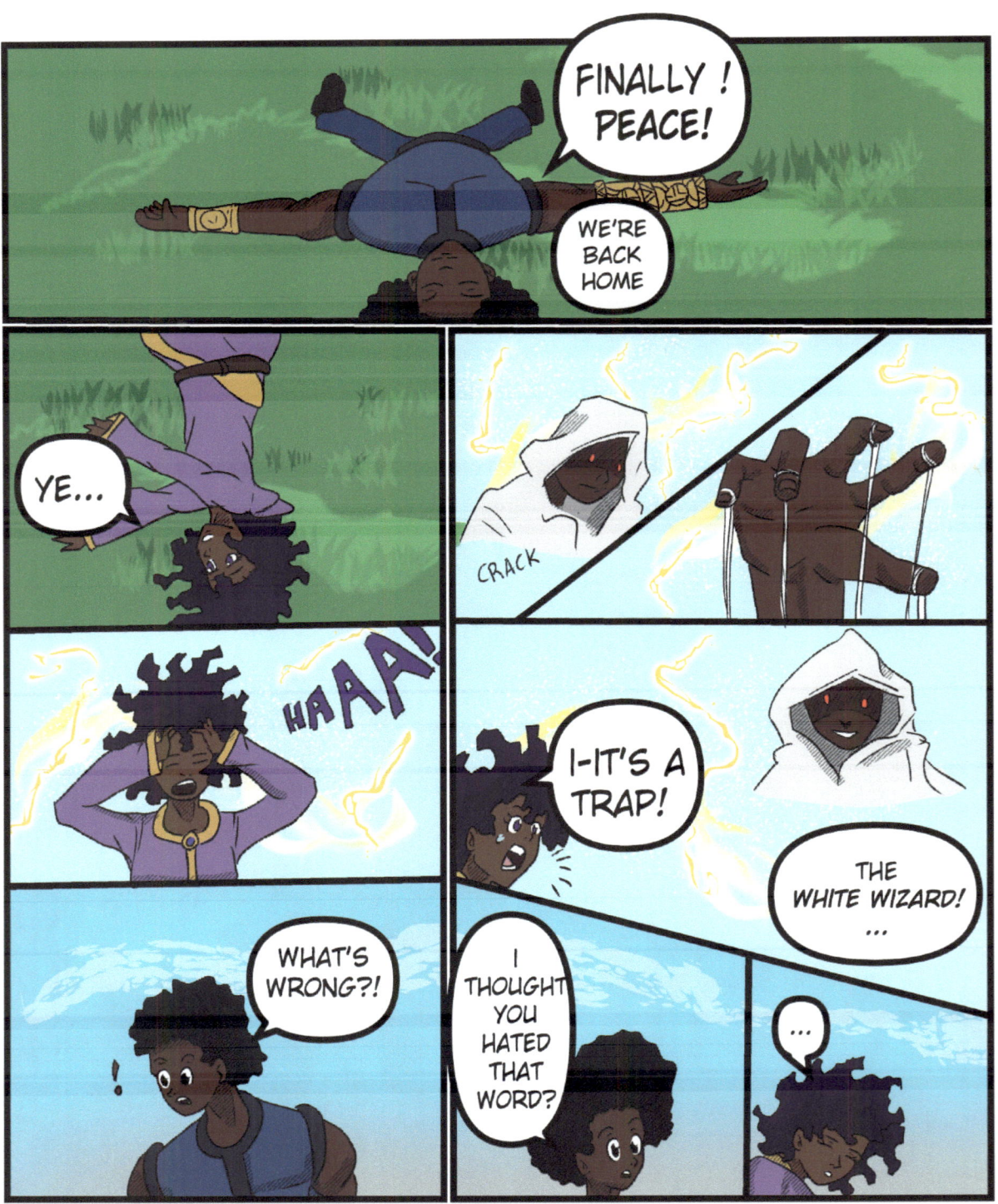

www.ingramcontent.com/pod-product-compliance
Lightning Source LLC
Chambersburg PA
CBHW041547240626
47164CB00003B/153